P9-DNE-287

Picture the Sky

BARBARA REID

Albert Whitman & Company
Chicago, Illinois

With thanks to artists—for what they see,
and how they share it

Library of Congress Cataloging-in-Publication data is on file with the publisher.

Published by arrangement with Scholastic Canada Limited
First published in Canada in 2017 by North Winds Press, an imprint of Scholastic Canada
First published in the United States of America in 2019 by Albert Whitman & Company
ISBN 978-0-8075-9525-1

The illustrations for this book were made with modelling clay
that was shaped and pressed onto illustration board.
Photography by Ian Crysler

Printed in China
10 9 8 7 6 5 4 3 2 1 WKT 22 21 20 19 18

For more information about Albert Whitman & Company,
visit our website at www.albertwhitman.com.

There is more than one
way to picture the sky.

It can be a blanket
or the curtain rising
on your day.

STOP

The sky can be an eyeful.

It can slip into
the background.

You can find it up,
down, or all around.

It can be a playground,
a highway, a home.

You can watch the passing parade.

You may find a story
in the sky,

or a weather report.

Did dinosaurs read the sky?

Can snowmen?

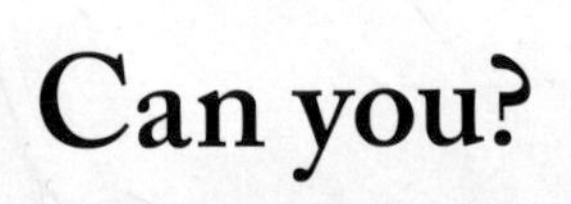

Can you?

There may be a sky
in your mind's eye.

Sometimes it's
movie night.

The sky can play hide-and-seek.

It may say: “Let’s dance!”

Artists see a masterpiece.

It's an ever-changing,
always open, everyone
welcome art gallery.

Wherever we are, we share the same sky.

It is the roof over our heads.

Picture the sky. How do you feel?

P9-DMW-334

by

Grace Lin

VIKING

FABER

Robert and his family lived in a house that looked a bit like a shoe. Really it was a boot, but Grandpa had made a lot of changes to it.

"The good thing about being small," Grandpa said to Robert, "is that it's easy to find things to patch the house with. Our poor house, every day it needs something. Oh well, what can you expect? It's a pretty old boot."

And it *was* a very old boot. The roof would leak and the kitchen would flood and the walls would crack. "Maybe we should look for a new home," Aunt Vicky sighed.

But when would they ever be able to find a new home before winter? For winter was always the worry. There had to be enough nuts and berries, firewood, blankets, and bedding; and all of it had to be gathered and stored. There was never enough time to look for a new house.

Right before the first snow, Robert's family sealed the windows and the doors shut. "We're not going to go outside anyway," Mum told Robert, "so we might as well seal everything to keep the snow out."

Rx Me
Take T

When the snow came, it covered the toe of the boot first, then the heel, and then the ankle. Slowly the whole boot was wrapped in snow, the door was blocked, and all the windows were filled, except for one.

That window belonged to Robert, who lived in the smallest room (because he was the smallest mouse) on the highest floor.

"Too much snow," Grandpa grumbled, as the wind shrieked. "Too wet. Too cold."

"Is it?" Robert asked. Robert had never touched snow. "I want to see."

"There's nothing to see!" Aunt Vicky scoffed. "Snow is just trouble."

"For big animals," Grandma said, "snow's no problem. They just stomp, stomp right through it. For small animals like us, well, if we go out there we'd be lost in two seconds."

"Small animals like us," Mum said, "don't like snow."

THE BELLA SEED COMPANY
BOSTON, MA
530721

“I like snow,” Robert said to himself one night while he gazed out the window. The rest of the family was sound asleep as Robert watched the snow float from the night sky.

“I wish I could go out in the snow,” Robert whispered to one particularly bright star.

29
USA
A

SWOOOSH! CRACK! A strong gust of wind burst through Robert's window and pushed him across the room. Robert looked up in a daze. The seal was broken! Robert ran to the window and stuck out his head.

He felt a snowflake fall. Whiteness sparkled in front of him.

Robert stretched his head out farther, breathing in the fresh coldness. The soft chilly breeze whispered to him inviting him out. Robert reached out a little more, and then a little more after that and . . .

WHOOPS! Robert slipped! Out the window Robert fell, down, down, down into the snow.

Robert sat up. Soft coldness was all around him. "I'm in the snow!" Robert gasped in disbelief. "I'm in the snow!" Joy bubbled through him, and he burst into laughter.

Snowflakes fell all around him. It was an incredible thing.

"I love snow!" Robert hugged the air. "Mum and Grandpa and everyone is so silly. Snow is wonderful!"

But as Robert turned back to go home, a fear froze his heart. Where was the house? All he saw was whiteness and wind. Robert remembered that, after all, he was a small animal. And to small animals, snow was not wonderful. Snow was scary.

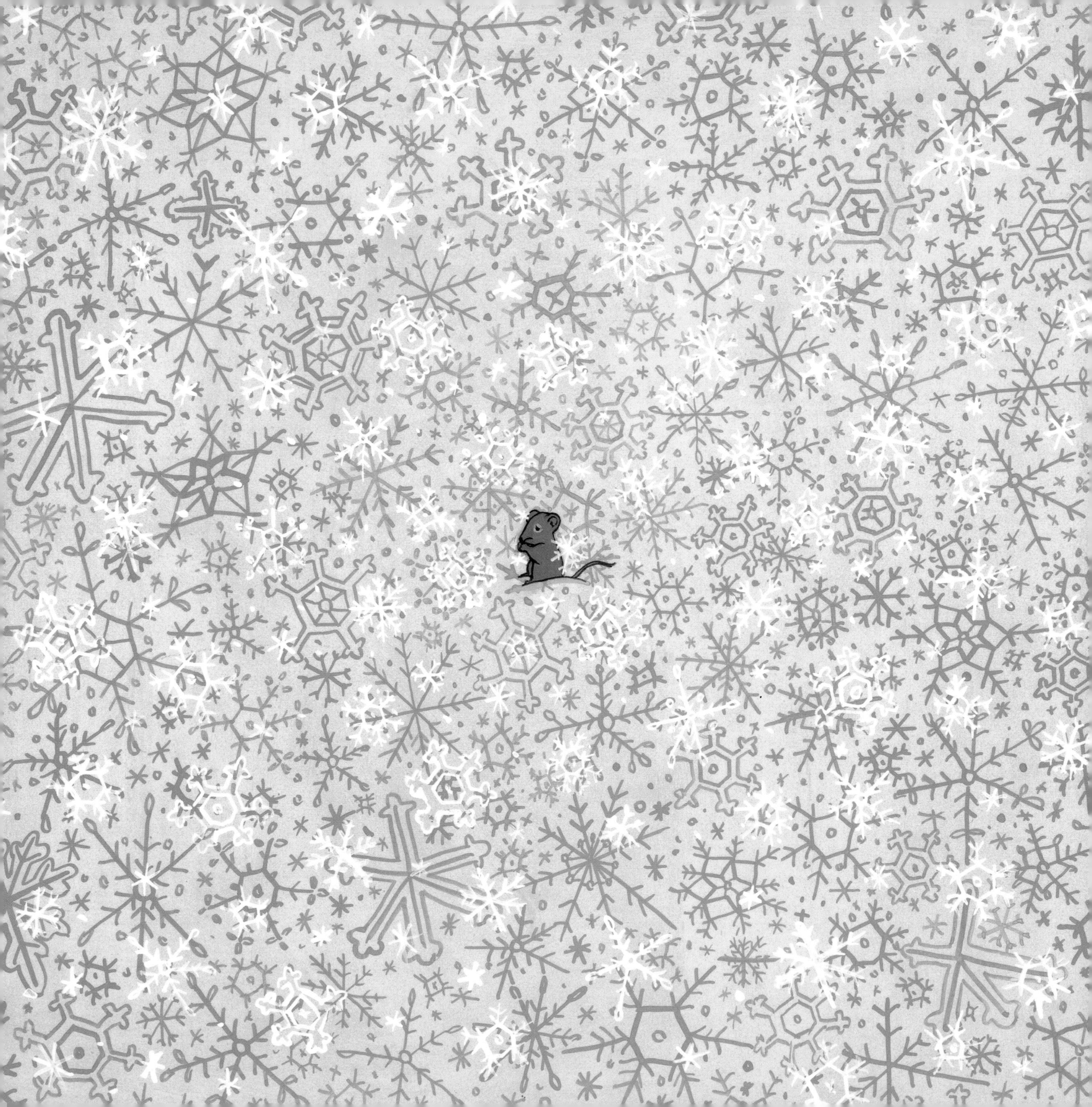

“What should I do?” Robert whispered. But no one answered. The wind howled, and the snow flew at him. Robert shivered. White, white, all around him was whiteness . . . and—wait! Red? Something red was in the snow. Robert squinted through the snowflakes. It was one of the big animals! One with red fur! And it was coming toward him.

"I have to hide!" Robert panicked. "It's coming!" He dug himself into the snow. His heart raced as he lay as still as he could underneath the snow. He could hear the big animal coming. *THUMP! THUMP!* With any luck, the big animal wouldn't notice something as small as Robert.

Poor Robert! In his haste to hide, he forgot to cover his tail!

The big animal stooped down and pulled Robert up, up, up out of the snow. It held Robert in the air and looked at him. The big animal wasn't all red, after all. It had red and white fur and big blue eyes. But it also had BIG teeth, because suddenly the animal opened his mouth and made a noise like thunder.

"HELP!" Robert screamed, and covered his face with his hands.

Robert felt himself being carried. He peeked through his fingers and saw the ground far below. It made him feel dizzy. Where was the big animal taking him?

Then Robert saw his house—the old boot, half covered with snow, with his window wide open. "Home," Robert whispered hopefully.

The big hand lowered him to his window and Robert jumped off. His room was so nice and warm, so safe and small! Robert ran to his bed and hugged his toys and his favorite blanket. Then he remembered the big animal.

USA 29
E

Carefully, Robert poked his head out the window. The big animal was leaving. "Thanks for bringing me back home!" Robert squeaked. The animal waved good-bye and walked away. Robert watched until the red disappeared into the whiteness of the falling snow.

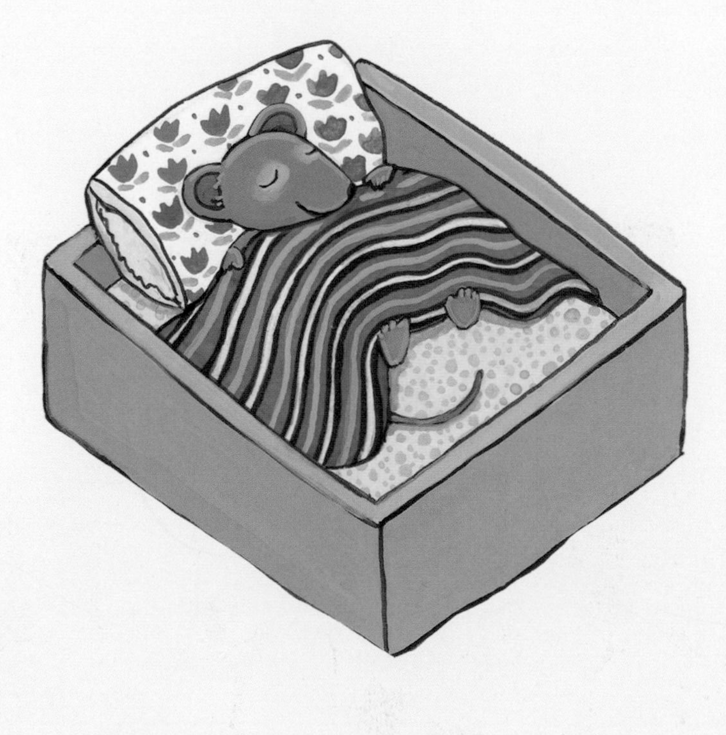

That spring, when the snow melted away, Robert's family finally unsealed the door.

"Thank goodness the snow is gone," Mum said.

"Now begins the endless repairs on the home," Grandpa sighed. But when he stepped outside, he stopped in shock. "By golly!" Grandpa said.

"What? What?" the rest of the family asked as they scrambled outside to join him.

33 USA
33 USA
33 USA
33 USA
7

Right next to their home 
was a brand-new boot—strong,
snug, and big enough for
the whole family. It
was a new home,
waiting for them.

"How on earth did it get here?" Grandma wondered. No one knew the answer.

But Robert could guess.

For Robert and the year we weren't allowed in the snow.

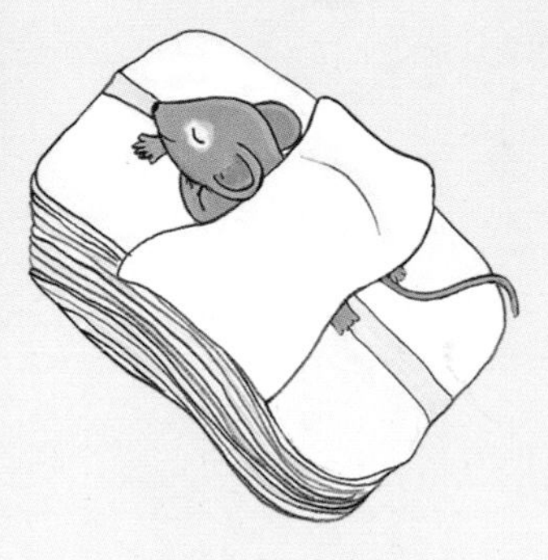

VIKING
Published by Penguin Group
Penguin Young Readers Group, 345 Hudson Street, New York, New York 10014, U.S.A.
Penguin Books Ltd, 80 Strand, London WC2R 0RL, England
Penguin Books Australia Ltd, 250 Camberwell Road, Camberwell, Victoria 3124, Australia
Penguin Books Canada Ltd, 10 Alcorn Avenue, Toronto, Ontario, Canada M4V 3B2
Penguin Books (N.Z.) Ltd, 182-190 Wairau Road, Auckland 10, New Zealand

First published in 2004 by Viking, a division of Penguin Young Readers Group

3 5 7 9 10 8 6 4 2

LIBRARY OF CONGRESS CATALOGING-IN-PUBLICATION DATA
Lin, Grace.
Robert's snow / by Grace Lin.
p. cm.
Summary: Robert, a little mouse anxious to experience snow, falls out of his bedroom window in his family's boot home and has a snow adventure.
ISBN 0-670-05911-0 (Hardcover)
[1. Mice—Fiction. 2. Snow—Fiction. 3. Home—Fiction.] I. Title.
PZ7.L644Ro 2004 [E]—dc22 2003025417

Manufactured in China Set in Cloister Bold Book design by Nancy Brennan